Miss Bindergarten Takes a Field Trip

with Kindergarten

by **JOSEPH SLATE**

illustrated by **ASHLEY WOLFF**

Dutton Children's Books · New York

For Milo Ryan,
Lane Smith,
and Greg Spaid—
three gracious steps

J.S.

For Donna Brooks,
Miss Bindergarten's right-paw woman

A.W.

CIP Data is available.

Published in the United States by Dutton Children's Books,
a division of Penguin Putnam Books for Young Readers
345 Hudson Street, New York, New York 10014
www.penguinputnam.com
First Edition   Printed in USA
2 4 6 8 10 9 7 5 3 1
ISBN 0-525-46710-6

Today is field trip day. . . .

Adam's dad's a chaperone.

Brenda's mom is, too.

Christopher says,
"Hey, don't leave yet—
a stone hopped
in my shoe."

Miss Bindergarten goes to the

bakery with kindergarten.

Danny cuts some cookies out.

Emily sees them bake.

Now Miss Bindergarten goes to the

fire station with kindergarten.

Gwen McGunny
rings a bell.

Henry holds
a hose.

Ian makes a funny face
and laughs as his nose groOOWS.

Jessie learns
Stop, Drop, and Roll.

Kiki tries
on gear.

Miss Bindergarten slides down the pole, and **L**enny gives a cheer.

Now Miss Bindergarten goes to the

post office with kindergarten.

Matty picks
the planet stamps.

Noah taps
the locks.

Ophelia asks where letters go when you slide them through the slots.

Patricia steers
a canvas cart.

Quentin checks
the scale.

Now Miss Bindergarten goes to the

library with kindergarten.

Sara grabs her favorite chair.

Tommy hugs a book.

Mr. Mack clicks the mouse.
"Here, **U**rsula, take a look!"

"A book is like a ticket
to all sorts of splendid trips."

Now Miss Bindergarten goes to the

park with kindergarten.

Xavier shouts,
"Where's Brenda's mom?"

Yolanda looks behind her.

"Don't worry. She's not lost,"
says **Z**ach.
"I know where we can find her."

Now Miss Bindergarten goes—whoa!

stops!—with kindergarten.

Adam's dad sets out the cups.

Brenda's mom pours punch.

Miss Bindergarten cuts the cake...

. . . and they all sit down

to munch!

Did you see these shapes?

we saw these shapes at the bakery

we saw these shapes at the fire station

circle

square

triangle

diamond

rectangle

we saw these shapes

we
saw these shapes

at the
post office

we
saw these shapes
at
the library

we saw these shapes

in
the park

hexagon

star

oval

heart

FRAGILE